Melzack, Ronald.

Raven, creator of the world. Eskimo legends retold by Ronald Melzack. Illustrated by László Gál. [1st American ed.] Boston, Little, Brown [1970]

91 p. col. illus. 25 cm. $4.95

A collection of ten Eskimo legends that relate how Raven, a superhuman being, created the world and animals and people.

1. Folklore, Eskimo
2. Eskimos—Legends. 2. Ravens—Legends and stories. [1. Eskimos—Legends. 3. Ravens—Stories] [1. Gál, László, illus.] I. Title.

WH 12/71

PZ8.1.M5Rav 3   398.24′09701   70–122535

MARC

Raven
Creator of the World

Eskimo Legends Retold by
Ronald Melzack

Illustrated by Laszlo Gal

Little, Brown and Company
Boston / Toronto

Contents

for
Lucy
Lauren
Joel

About Eskimo Legends

People of all cultures have a story to tell of the Creation of the World. The Bible of the Jewish and Christian people, for example, tells us that the god Jehovah made the world in six days and rested on the seventh, and that he did all this about six thousand years ago. The Mende tribe of Sierra Leone in Africa also believe that a god made the world, and that the god invited man to come to him for all his needs. But people pestered the god so much that he went high into the heavens, and man has never been able to communicate with him from that time on. The Chinese people have a different story to tell. They believe that the universe always existed but that it was in a state of Chaos until the two Emperors Shu and Hu destroyed Chaos with a bolt of lightning, created order, and thus made the world as we know it now.

Among the Eskimos there is yet another story of the way the world began. Raven, it is said, who can take the shape of a bird or a man, created the world, the animals, and people. This story of Creation is told primarily by Alaskan Eskimos. But there are additional Raven stories that are told by Eskimo communities across the whole northland. Taken together, these stories reveal a fascinating character – a super-human being to be admired for his creative powers and ingenuity, yet with human qualities that evoke sympathy and affection. The stories do still more: they tell us how Eskimos lived long ago, and how they perceived the world around them.

The Eskimo people derive originally from Asia, and, in a series of migrations across Alaska and northern Canada, settled in many different Arctic areas. They have survived for thousands of years, despite the cold and bleak terrain, and developed a unique culture that is superbly adapted to its environment. They call themselves "Innuit," which means simply "the people." We know them as "Eskimos," an Indian name which means "Eaters-of-raw-meat." The climate varies from one place to another in the Arctic northland, and each Eskimo community has developed its own way of life. The Eskimos near the North Pole, before they were taught to build houses, spent most of the year in igloos. Eskimos in warmer areas, such as the Bering Strait shores, live in tents or larger wooden houses. The vegetation also varies from one area to the next so that some Eskimos in Alaska enjoy having plants, berries, grass, and trees, while many Eskimos in northern Canada, before the recent technological development of the Arctic, had never seen a tree – indeed, tiny moss plants may have been all the vegetation they ever knew.

Since Eskimos had no written language before Western man entered their territory, their legends and traditions were handed down from generation to generation by word of mouth. We know their early stories only from the records kept by anthropologists and explorers. However, good Eskimo storytellers wanted, above all, to entertain. And that also is the purpose of these tales. . . .

How Raven Created The World

In the beginning, there was only Raven and the falling snowflakes.

Raven sailed through the soft silvery glow of the universe which stretched endlessly around him. Sparkling snowflakes swirled past him and tumbled around in circles as his wings swayed ever so slightly.

Once, Raven caught some snowflakes on his outstretched wings. He lowered one wing, and the snowflakes trickled down to his wingtip and made a little snowball. He amused himself as he flew, gently lowering and raising his wing, and watched the little snowball grow as it rolled back and forth. Then, with a great sweep of his wing, he hurled the snowball through the air.

Raven watched, fascinated, as his snowball soared across the sky, picking up more snowflakes as it hurtled along. It grew larger and larger until it was immense. Raven flew after it, sailed above it, and then lowered himself gently onto it. He stretched out his legs and realized that he had never before stood on solid ground. He had been flying for as long as he could remember, and it felt good to rest his wings.

Raven felt an itch near his beak. He scratched it and, to his astonishment, his beak moved! He pushed it up so that it sat on his forehead. His wings felt strange, and, as he moved them, his wing-cape slipped off his shoulders. He stood upright on two legs and moved his hands slowly over his face. He felt his eyes, his nose, his mouth. His fingers examined the beak on his forehead.

The soft, white snow-hills sparkled in the pale, silvery light. Raven kicked away at the snow with his foot, and soon he saw rich brown clay. He picked up the clay and moulded little seeds out of it. Then Raven swept his wing-cape across his shoulders, lowered his beak, and flew from place to place and planted the seeds. Wherever he planted them a forest grew up – tree after tree, with herbs and plants around their roots. Raven thought this new land was beautiful and he called it Earth. The place he came from he called the Sky.

Raven liked Earth and each day he flew to see all the things he had created. He wandered through the forests and tended the plants and flowers, especially the tiny shoots that sprang out of the earth and grew slowly upward.

One plant grew quickly, so quickly that Raven could actually see it grow. Leaves sprouted out of the plant, and little buds near the leaves grew into pea-pods.

As he watched, he saw a pea-pod move and jiggle, yet there was no wind. It shook and quivered and then it split open, and a little living creature popped out. It jumped around and kicked the snow. The creature was cold, and, as it jumped up and down, its teeth chattered.

Raven went up to the newcomer and smiled. "Who are you?" he asked.

"I came from that pod," said the creature. "I was tired of lying there, so I kicked out a hole and jumped through!"

Raven laughed heartily. "You're a funny fellow! You look a little familiar, though I've never seen you before!" And he laughed again. "I created that pod plant myself, but I had no idea that you would jump out."

"And where did *you* come from?" asked the little creature.

"I have always been here," said Raven. "Come to think of it, you look a lot like me, except that you don't have a beak on your forehead. I will call you Man and I will be your friend." Raven plucked feathers from his wing-cape and made a little parka for Man to wear and keep his body warm.

That was how the first man was created, and Raven

watched many more men, and women too, hop out of the pea-pod plant.

Raven fed the people with berries from the plants that he had grown. But the people needed more food. And so Raven made the animals and he made them of clay. After he had fashioned them in the shapes that delighted him, he set the clay creatures out to dry in the cool air. And when they had dried out, Raven called the people to behold what he had made. The people thought they were beautiful. Then Raven told the people to close their eyes. He pulled his beak down over his mouth, and waved his wings five times over the shapes. Soon they started to breathe and move. They were alive. Raven raised his mask and told the people to look. When they saw the animals moving, full of life, they cried out with pleasure. Raven experimented with these creatures until they looked just right to him. And that is how he learned to make every kind of animal, fish, and bird, and he taught each kind to live on the earth, in the sea, or in the air.

Raven showed the animals to the people and said that some animals would be their food as soon as people learned to hunt. But that would not be easy, because the pale, silvery glow of the sky was just enough for people to see things close at hand. When men wanted to walk to distant places, they had to grope about with their hands and find things out by listening.

Men heard the howling of the wolves, the grunting of the bears, and the growling of the foxes. In the sea the seals snorted, the walruses wheezed, the whales blew. Birds whistled and sang, insects hummed. Men heard, too, the whispering of the winds, the rustle and murmur of the leaves, and the surging of the surf against the shore.

Raven loved all the creatures he had created, but there were none that he respected or admired more than the sparrows. One day, he called a little sparrow and said to her, "Far off in the universe lies the source of all light. Even though you are small and plain, you are the hardiest and bravest creature of all. Therefore I command you to fly out into the universe and bring back Light so that people may see the world, the animals, and one another."

The little sparrow flew off and stayed away in the darkness until Raven thought she would never come back. At last, he heard the whirr of her wings and felt her floating down and settling on his hand. The sparrow carried three little packets in her beak, each wrapped in a leaf. She gave them to Raven.

Raven opened one of the leaves and saw a ball of brilliant, dazzling gold. He called it the Sun. He threw it into the air, and immediately a great radiance filled the earth and dazzled everyone. For the first time, people could see the earth on which they lived. They saw the woods, the animals on land and in the sea, and the birds in the air. They rejoiced at all the beauty around them. Life became a new and greater thing for all of them. When the sun set, Raven opened another leaf, and in it was a ball of iron. Raven threw it up into the air and called it the Moon. Raven called the light of the sun Day and the light of the moon Night, and both the sun and the moon have gracefully shared the sky with each other ever since.

Now people were happy. Raven taught them to build igloos

and tents to shelter themselves from the wind and the storms. He taught them to make kayaks and big boats so that they could sail on the sea and hunt the sea-creatures. He taught them to make spears and other weapons to hunt the animals that roam the land. And he showed them how to build a fire to warm themselves when they were cold, and to cook the meat when it was too tough to eat.

Men and animals flourished on earth and their numbers kept increasing. But the land was too small to hold them all. One day, Raven said to the people, "So that there may be food and space enough for all, the old must henceforth make way for the young." And for the first time, the oldest of all living things – people and animals, plants and trees – weakened and died. Yet men and animals continued to flourish, and their numbers kept increasing.

One day, Raven moulded clay to make new kinds of animals for his people. The clay was too wet, and when he set it out to dry, it all ran together and made a huge serpent unlike any other animal. The serpent slithered down to the sea, and swam around near shore, waiting to pounce on the men in their boats. Men rode up to it in their kayaks and tried to harpoon it, but all the harpoons bounced off its sides.

Raven saw the hopeless struggle and said to the little sparrow, who followed him everywhere, "Fly out and hover above the serpent while I hunt it from my kayak." Then Raven followed the sparrow to the serpent.

The sparrow glided above the serpent and inspected it intently. Soon she pointed to its soft belly, and Raven threw

his harpoon. The serpent exploded with a tremendous roar. The men shouted with joy as they watched bits of serpent fly up into the air and then come crashing down into the sea, where they turned into islands. Land shot up near land, and the whole became a wide and spacious coast. In this way, new land was created and there was enough room on earth for everybody, men and animals too.

One day, just after the sun had gone down and the sky was a deep, rich blue, Raven gathered all the people and said to them, "I am your Creator. To me you owe your lives and your land, and you must never forget me."

Raven drew his beak down over his mouth and swept his wing-cape across his shoulders. He spread his wings wide and sailed up to the sky, where it was dark. In one wing he held the last of the leaves that the sparrow had given him. He shook open the leaf, and in it were little pieces of silver. He threw the silver pieces into the air, and they scattered across the whole sky. Raven called them the Stars. The people were enchanted by the tiny, glittering lights, and they sang out in awe and delight.

And this was the way Raven made the earth, the men, and the animals, and the sun, the moon, and the stars.

Raven
And The Goose

Raven flew above the earth and he liked what he had made. He saw the men hunt and the women gather berries, and he rejoiced in their happiness. He watched the boys and girls grow into splendid men and women. The men and the women married, and Raven took delight in their children.

The people and the animals flourished, and they lived together in harmony. The trees and plants and flowers spread across the earth, and the oceans were full of whales and seals and fish. All the living creatures that Raven made knew happiness and love. Each creature found its mate, and both grew old together until they died. But Raven was immortal. He lived on and on, and all the things he loved grew old and died.

Raven was lonely, and one day he returned to earth to live among his people and to share in their happiness. Raven wanted to marry. He searched everywhere for a girl who would become his wife. At last, he saw a little sparrow. The sparrow was crying, and Raven settled down beside her.

"Why are you crying?" he asked her.

"I am crying for my husband, who is lost," she answered. "I love him because he catches worms for me."

"It's not right for you to cry," said Raven. "Take me for your husband. I have a high forehead and a big beak. You will sleep under my wing, and I will give you dainty centipedes to eat."

"No, thank you," said the little sparrow to Raven, who towered above her. "My husband may yet return. Besides, centipedes are too pretty to eat."

So Raven flew away.

Raven flew on and soon he saw a small snowbird. The snowbird was crying and Raven asked her why she wept.

"I am crying for my husband," she said. "He has been away such a long time. He flew off to look for food for me, and he hasn't yet come back."

"Your husband is probably gone forever," Raven said. "But don't worry, I will marry you. You can sleep under my wing. Take me for a husband! I have a pretty beak, and a handsome chin. I have good nostrils and eyes, and my wings are strong and broad."

But the little snowbird said, "Thank you for your kindness, but I'm sure my husband will return."

Raven grew sad and flew off again.

One summer day Raven decided that, if he could not find himself a wife, he would make one. And so he took some clay and moulded it into an egg. He set the egg down in soft grass and cared for it. He warmed the egg when the air was cold, and he turned it over from time to time. At last, the egg began to move. Raven watched it jiggle and shake until a little beak pushed through the top of the egg. He watched with joy, for at last he would have the woman he wanted. The beak sawed up and down and opened the top of the eggshell. A little head pushed through and Raven stared in amazement. Instead of a raven, it was a goose!

Raven looked after the little goose, brought her food, and watched her grow up. He named her Anana. He helped her pluck her gray, downy feathers and watched beautiful, white feathers grow in their place. Her wing feathers grew in slender and strong, and soon she was able to fly. Then Raven and Anana flew off together across the cold northland.

One day, they saw a flock of geese, and Anana said, "These are my people. I must join them. Come with me." Raven loved Anana, and together they joined the flock of geese and lived with them.

When the days became shorter and colder, the leader of

the flock came to Anana and Raven, and said, "Tomorrow we must begin our long journey south. We will fly across the land and the waters until we reach the warmer country where we may live." Raven wanted to fly with Anana, but she said, "You are too heavy to come with us. You will not be able to follow us when we fly across the sea. There is no place for you to rest. If you grow tired, you will fall into the water and drown."

But Raven was obstinate. "Nothing in the world can tire me," he said loftily. And so, in the end, Anana agreed.

Before they left, Raven put his wing tenderly around Anana. But she drew away, and said, "I have grown too fond of you, and my grief will be too heavy when I lose you during our flight across the sea."

"Don't worry," said Raven proudly. "I once flew for an eternity of time without tiring!"

"True," said Anana, "but you haven't flown much lately. You've been so busy making the world and looking after it."

Raven smiled knowingly at Anana and put his wing around her again.

The next day, the geese set out and Raven flew with them. Soon they came to the end of the land and stopped. They settled down to rest before their journey across the great sea.

Anana said to Raven, "Now rest here so that you will not be tired while you cross the sea."

"I thrive on activity," said Raven boastfully. And he flew up high above the geese to admire the sweep of the coast.

After the geese had rested, they rose and flew out across the sea. When they were half-way across, Raven became very tired. Sometimes he beat his wings wildly and almost fell into the sea. But his wings were still strong enough to raise him again.

They had not far to go to land, when Raven cried out for help. He was very tired, and could go no further.

Anana and another goose then swam on the water, and each spread out her wing. Anana's right wing covered her friend's left wing, and both together made a bridge on which Raven rested.

Raven was tired, and after a little while he dropped slowly through the wing-bridge: not all at once, but little by little. First his feet slipped through. Then the water came up to his chest, then to his wings, to his neck, to his chin.

"I must go," called Anana's friend, "before our flock is out of sight." And she flew off.

Anana pulled Raven to a piece of ice which floated in the water. Raven rested his chin on it, while she, weeping, tried to hold up his head.

But Raven was too heavy and too tired. The ice gave way and many bubbles rose up when Raven sank. Anana wept. She wanted to stay with Raven, but the honking calls of the flock were irresistible. "Good-bye," she called to Raven. And she went on her way with the other geese.

Raven felt himself sinking deeper into the water. With all his strength, he flapped his wings and pushed himself towards the surface. He breathed again and looked around. Wistfully, he watched Anana and all the geese flying away from him. He struggled to rise from the water, to join his Anana, but his wings were soaked, and he drifted back and forth. After a long time, a great wave cast him on shore.

The water ran in streams from Raven's soaked feathers, and his wings dragged on the ground. He fell several times, until at last he reached some bushes. He held on to a bush for a moment and then, with one wing, pushed up his beak. His wing-cape fell off his shoulders and he stood on the beach, shivering in the cold. He draped his wing-cape across a bush. He found some driftwood, and soon he had a fire burning. He searched the horizon, but there was no sign of Anana.

Raven felt sad and lonely as he stood in front of the fire. He jumped slowly up and down, trying to warm himself. And, as he jumped, his feet danced out a little rhythm on the rocks. Raven danced faster and faster and, as he warmed up, he felt happier. He began to sing to himself, as he danced around the fire, and his arms swayed gracefully in time with his feet. He lifted his wing-cape and it swirled around and around as he danced. Soon he swept his cape across his shoulders, and his wings rose high as he danced a wild and happy rhythm in the loneliness of the beach.

When the fire went out, Raven lowered his beak, and flew off to return to his people.

Raven And
The Keewak Bird

Raven lived with his people and shared their happiness. But he was still lonely.

"How good it would be to have a friend to fly with," he thought to himself.

One day, he moulded some clay into an egg, and watched and cared for it. Soon it began to move, and Raven heard a sweet-sounding "cheep-cheep" inside the shell. A crack appeared near the top of the egg, and a funny, crooked beak pushed through. It sawed around the top of the shell, and then a bird popped out. It was a Keewak bird!

"Welcome to the world!" exclaimed Raven.

"And hello to you," said the bird. "Who are you?"

"I am Raven. I made you. I also made the Earth you're standing on."

The Keewak bird stared at Raven. He cocked his head to one side and looked at him through one eye. He shrugged his wings slightly, and began to preen his feathers as they dried out in the sunshine.

Raven inspected the Keewak bird. He had a twisted, crooked beak, and each eye was a different colour – one was yellow, the other was blue. One wing was slightly bigger than the other, and he had thick tufts of feathers on his chest and on the top of his head.

The bird shook and fluffed his feathers, then looked up and saw Raven inspecting him.

"Why did you make me?" he asked.

"Because I want a friend to fly with," said Raven.

"Fly? What's that?"

"Watch," said Raven, and he gave a hop, spread his wings, and lifted off the ground. He flew around directly above the Keewak bird's head, and called down to him, "Join me – it's beautiful up here."

"How?" asked the bird.

"It's easy. Give a little hop, spread your wings, and the wind will take care of the rest."

The bird gave a little hop, spread his wings, and before he knew it he was up in the air.

"Help, help!" he cried. "I'll fall down and break into little pieces."

"No! No!" called Raven. "Just keep flying! You'll see – it's fun!"

The Keewak bird flapped his wings and flew, and it was fun.

Soon Raven flew closer to the bird, and they both glided through the air. Raven was happy as the wind rushed past his face. It was cool and fresh, and he felt content. He swooped down and rose suddenly up again. He frolicked through the air as the Keewak bird watched.

The Keewak bird tried to frolic too and, as he watched Raven flying somersaults and loop-the-loops, he too felt happy. He flew alongside Raven. They glided gracefully through the air, feeling the warmth of silent companionship, then – suddenly – they crashed into each other and fluttered down to earth.

Raven picked himself up and helped the Keewak bird to his feet.

"You turned the wrong way!" he said gently. "Let's try again."

"Let's rest," said the Keewak bird. "Flying is dangerous, and I don't think we should overdo it."

"No! No!" said Raven. "If you fall out of the sky, then it's important to fly again immediately."

So up they flew.

"Now," said Raven, "I'll teach you how to fly. First lesson: if you want to turn right, lower your right wing and raise your left; but if you want to turn left, lower your left wing and raise your right."

"Which is my right wing and which is my left wing?" asked the Keewak bird.

"Your right wing is on the right side of your body and your left wing is on the left side," said Raven.

"But which is the left and which is the right side?"

Raven pointed with one wing, and said, "*That* is your left," and he pointed to the Keewak bird's other wing and said, "that is your right. Now remember what I said and let's turn left right now!"

Crash! They both fell to earth. Raven picked himself up, looked around and saw two feet kicking in the air. He ran over, and there was the Keewak bird, his beak wedged into the earth, and his feet and wings fluttering upwards.

Raven grasped the bird's feet firmly, and tugged and pulled. Suddenly his beak came free, and they both went flying up into the air, twisting around and around as they went.

"Spread your wings," called Raven.

The Keewak bird spread his wings.

"Where am I? What happened? Who hit me?" he cried.

"I can see," said Raven, "that teaching you to tell left from right won't be easy. Well, I didn't make the world in a day, and it's clear, too, that you're not going to learn left from right in a day. So now, Lesson two: to fly back down to earth, sweep your wings upward and move your tail downward, and you'll float down. Let's go."

The Keewak bird said, "Let me get it straight – my wings go up and my tail goes down, right?"

"Perfect," said Raven.

Alas, the Keewak bird did not know up from down any better than he knew left from right. He gathered up all his energy and swept his wings down and lifted his tail up. And with a mighty swoop, he zoomed straight up into the air.

"Come back, my dear, new friend," Raven called after him. But the Keewak bird flew up with such speed that he got smaller and smaller, and he soon shot right out of sight.

And neither Raven nor anyone else has ever again seen a Keewak bird.

Raven
And The Whale

One evening, while the sun was setting, Raven flew along the seashore to watch the ever-changing colours of the waves. As he scanned the horizon, he caught sight of fountains of water rising up from the distant sea. The water shot up high, foamed and bubbled, and fell back on the sea. Raven was curious and flew toward the sparkling, foaming fountains. Soon he was close enough to see a school of whales, each whale spouting a stream of bubbly water.

Raven soared above the whales and, to his surprise, saw a faint glow of light coming from one of the whales each time it opened its mouth. He flew closer to the whale to see where the light came from. Each time the whale's mouth opened, Raven flew a little closer – the light was mysterious, yet it looked warm and inviting. Just as Raven was inspecting the light, the whale lurched forward and swallowed him.

Raven looked around. The whale's spine above him resembled a strong and beautiful roof, and the delicate ribs formed graceful arches, like the walls of a great house. He listened, and heard the rhythmic beat of the whale's heart. Raven lifted his beak and walked swiftly toward the light, his wing-cape swirling behind him. Then he stopped suddenly in astonishment. In the center of the whale was a softly glowing lamp, and beside the lamp stood the most beautiful girl he had ever seen. The dancing flame-light made her face glow, and Raven was enchanted.

The girl looked at Raven and smiled shyly. Raven moved closer. The lamp flame fluttered ceaselessly – it rose and fell, rose and fell. Its dancing light radiated warmth and beauty, and the girl's white teeth dazzled Raven's eyes as he watched her. When he approached a little, Raven saw that the girl was dancing on her toes. Her legs barely moved, while her body and arms swayed slowly in rhythm to the loud beats of the whale's heart. Raven watched her supple, graceful movements, and noticed that the tips of her toes flowed from a delicate thread that was attached to the whale's beating heart.

Raven was overwhelmed with love for the girl as he watched her dance.

Finally, Raven asked, "Who are you?"

"I am the whale's spirit," said the girl.

"I love you," said Raven, "Come with me and be my wife."

The girl laughed sweetly, and her laughter echoed through the whale.

"I cannot leave," she said, dancing while she talked. "The whale and I are one, and I must look after the lamp. It warms us and keeps us alive in the freezing water."

"But you are too beautiful to spend your life inside a whale, dancing every moment, yet never moving anywhere."

"I am the whale's spirit," said the girl, "and I cannot leave. Besides, I love this lamp, and it makes me happy."

"Then take the lamp with you," said Raven.

"No," said the girl. "The lamp must stay where it is, and you must never touch it." She smiled at Raven and continued, "I am pleased to have a friend, and you may stay as long as you wish. But you must never, never touch my lamp."

Raven watched the girl, and a deep sadness overcame him. "How beautiful she is," he thought to himself. "How graceful and delicate and sweet. How happy I would be if she became my wife!"

As Raven looked around, he saw an opening above him. It was the whale's spout, and Raven could see the stars when he looked straight through it. Slowly, a plan formed in his mind.

When the whale began to sleep in the still blackness of the night, the girl's dance became slower and sleepier. Her eyelids shut from time to time, and she seemed to sleep even while she danced. Raven waited, watching – then, the moment her eyes closed, he snatched up the lamp of life, swept the girl into his arms, and snapped her free from the delicate thread. He dashed toward the spout.

But too late!

The whale suddenly lurched up and thrashed around. Raven and the girl fell backwards. The lamp flickered, grew fainter, and died out. Raven held the girl tightly in his arms, but she became smaller and lost her shape. She no longer moved and became tinier and tinier.

"Come back to me!" he called. "I will make you my wife and look after you as long as you live."

But Raven heard only the sea waves swirling around him as the girl vanished into nothingness.

The whale suddenly stopped moving. Raven looked up and saw the sky through the whale's spout. He lowered his beak and flew up, and in a moment he was high above the whale. It was dead, and had washed up on shore. Raven flew down to the shore, sat on a rock, and looked at the whale.

"How beautiful is the spirit of a whale," he whispered to himself.

White-capped waves rushed up on shore. The salty mist made Raven's eyes smart, and tears rolled down his face as he stared at the whale. He watched it for many hours as it rocked gently back and forth with the inrushing and outgoing tide.

Raven
And The Seals

Raven sat on the icy shore, huddled up, his chin on his knees. He watched the lifeless whale in front of him, as it rocked back and forth. The sun was rising quickly above the horizon and it warmed him and dried the sea-spray on his feather-cape.

While he was sitting and dozing in the warm sun, he heard "splash, swish-swish; splash, swish-swish." As the sound grew louder he scanned the horizon and, down the shore, he saw an army of seals leaping out of the water and marching toward him. They walked on their tails and, as they marched, their flippers swayed back and forth, and went "swish-swish, swish-swish."

When they were close to the whale, their leader marched up to Raven and announced, "We are here for our breakfast. We are going to eat the large fish on the beach."

"What?" exclaimed Raven. "Eat the woman I love? Never!"

The seals looked at Raven, and Raven looked back at the seals.

"But we're hungry," cried the seals.

Raven suddenly had an idea.

"Whale is a great delicacy," he explained, "and there's a special way to eat one – from the top down. Follow me."

The leader of the seals raised his head, puffed up his chest, wiggled his whiskers, and barked, "Attention! Forward! March!" And the army of seals marched behind Raven. Raven jumped on top of the whale, and the seals tried to do the same. They leapt up the side of the whale, and then slid down, falling on their flippers, their noses, and their sides. They bumped into each other, crashed against one another, and cried, "Where's the food?"

Finally, Raven called, "Wait! I know another way to eat a whale – from the inside out. I'll open the whale's mouth and let you in. But it's dark in there. Wait for me, and be patient. I'll be right back with special medicine that will make you see in the dark." Raven immediately pulled down his beak, put on his wing-cape, and flew off.

Raven flew south. He soared across the ice and snow until he saw the first trees of the forest. He flew to the closest spruce tree, ran his wing across the spruce tree's branches, and collected a ball of the sticky gum that covers them. When he had enough, he flew back to the whale.

"I'm back," Raven called, and all the seals cheered. "I have the magic medicine to rub into your eyes that will make you see in the dark. Now walk up to me one by one."

The seals jumped to attention and lined up in single file. As they marched past Raven, he rubbed the sticky gum over their eyelids and stuck them together.

"I can't see," said the leader of the seals.

"You will," said Raven, "just follow me into the whale."

"Lead us to the food," cried the seals.

"This way," announced Raven. He whistled a merry tune, and the seals marched – swish-swish, swish-swish – behind him.

Instead of leading the seals into the whale, Raven marched south. The seals cried out, "How warm it is in the whale!"

"Just normal," cried Raven. "Follow me and don't stop."

So Raven walked south, and the seals marched after him in single file.

"We still can't see," said the seals.

"Don't worry," said Raven. "It's dark in the whale. Just keep marching until you see the light."

Raven suddenly flew up, sailed high above the seals, and watched them marching south. Their tails wiggled back and forth, and went swish-swish, swish-swish. Raven watched them until they marched out of sight.

As the seals marched south, the sun grew warmer, and some exclaimed, "It's too hot inside the whale! Let's turn back."

"No!" shouted the leader. "Forward, to victory and to food!"

And they marched – swish-swish – and marched – swish-swish – and marched – swish-swish.

At last, the hot sun melted the sticky gum on their eyelids, and they beheld the world around them.

"How spacious and beautiful it is inside the whale," one said.

"Look! Straight ahead!" another one called. "That's where the food must be!"

And they all ran ahead – into the forest.

The wolves and foxes snarled, the bears grunted, the small animals growled and howled, the owls hooted, the birds screeched, and the deer crashed through the bushes.

The seals' eyes opened wide in terror!

"Let's get out of the whale," one called. "It's full of devils and evil spirits."

The seals dashed away from the forest and ran all the way back to the sea.

From that day on, it is said, seals eat only little fish – and scurry away whenever they see a whale!

Raven
And The Fox

The snow was falling, and Raven knew that winter was coming. He cut snowblocks with his long knife and put them together to make an igloo. He built a short tunnel in front of the entrance to keep out the cold wind and put blocks of ice on two sides to make the windows of his home. Raven went out to hunt each day, and in the evening he returned with his food. His little oil lamp gave him warmth and light, and he used its heat to warm the meat in his pot.

Raven lived alone, and he was lonely. When he left each

morning for the day's hunt, his igloo was always in a messy state. The fur blankets of his bed lay rumpled on the floor, and his feather-cape, his parka, and other clothing lay scattered about.

One day, when Raven returned home, he found that his igloo was clean and beautiful. The blankets lay neatly on the bed, and his wing-cape was set out beside it. Raven realized that someone must have come into his igloo, but he could not imagine who it might have been.

The next day, when Raven returned home after a long, tiring hunt, he again found that his igloo was exquisitely clean. His wing-cape had been brushed, and it shone in the sparkling light of the oil-lamp. His blanket lay smoothly across the bed, and his clothes were folded neatly beside it.

Raven ate his food, and decided that he must find out who had been visiting his igloo.

The next day, Raven prepared to set out to hunt, but instead of going far away, he hid behind a nearby snowbank. He waited for many hours and then, suddenly, he saw a beautiful young fox trot up to his igloo, and walk into the tunnel. Raven waited, and, after a while, the fox trotted out again. As soon as the fox had disappeared from sight, Raven ran into his igloo and again he found it clean and neat.

The next day, Raven again hid behind the snowbank. He waited for a long time and, finally, he saw the fox trot up to his igloo and run through the tunnel. Raven waited a few moments, and then ran into the igloo himself. There he saw a fox skin lying beside his own feather-cape. And, standing near the oil-lamp, was an exquisite girl sewing a patch on his parka. Raven smiled happily as he examined her pretty, oval face, her big bright eyes, and her long, shining black braids.

The moment the girl saw Raven, she ran to get her fox skin and started to put it on. But Raven stopped her. "Wait," he said. "I am thankful to you for looking after my igloo while I am away hunting."

"But I must leave," cried the Fox-girl.

"No," said Raven, "you must stay and you must become my wife. You are lovely, and you have been very good to me. I will do everything I can to make you happy."

"How can you possibly love me," asked the girl. "I smell like a fox, and everyone knows that foxy smells are terrible."

"No," said Raven. "I don't notice the way you smell. I see only that you are beautiful and kind. You must stay with me and be my wife."

The Fox-girl thought for a moment, and then she agreed. "I will stay with you as long as you are happy with me," she said, "but promise me that no one will ever mention that I smell different from any other creature."

Raven promised her.

"My name is Mavarana," she said.

And that day Mavarana became Raven's wife.

Raven and Mavarana lived happily for a long time. Each morning Raven went out to hunt, and, when he returned in the evening, his igloo was always clean and lovely. There was always food in the pot, and Raven and Mavarana sat together silently, eating their food and feeling happy in the warmth of

the igloo. Raven brought home animal skins, and Mavarana made clothes to keep him warm. She dried the skins, and chewed them with her teeth to make them pliable and soft. And with her needle she sewed the skins together and made Raven the most beautiful clothes anyone had ever seen. The Eskimos of the nearby village were astonished at how handsome Raven had become. He dressed better than anyone else, and he looked happier than ever before.

"Let us meet your wife," the Eskimo people asked Raven.

"No," said Raven. "She is mine alone. I am happy with her, and no one but I shall know her."

One day, while Raven and Mavarana ate their evening meal, there was a noise outside their igloo. Just as Raven was about to get up, in marched Owl. His long, sharp beak bobbed up and down as he walked.

"My, it's cold out there," said Owl. "A perfectly miserable night. It's good to see you again, Raven! I shall be staying with you for several days."

Raven and Mavarana looked at each other. They began to think of ways to get Owl out of the igloo, but they could think of none. It was cold and snowing outside and Raven could not ask Owl to leave on such a terrible night.

"My, your food smells wonderful, Raven," said Owl. "What a lucky man you are to have such a marvellous wife."

Raven beamed with pleasure.

Owl ate the meat that was given to him, snapping up each piece with his long beak. Then he asked for more, and still more, until Raven and Mavarana were completely out of food.

Then Owl said, "My, your bed looks soft and warm and inviting! Naturally you are going to ask me to join you in your bed!"

And so Raven and Mavarana and Owl all slept that night in the same bed.

The next morning, as Raven was preparing for the day's hunt, Owl said, "I think I will stay and help your little wife look after your home."

Raven went off and came back as quickly as he could. He had caught two seals, and decided that they would be enough for the three of them for supper that night.

When Raven came into the house, Owl was standing in front of the oil lamp, warming his wings.

"Raven," said Owl, "yours is a wonderful home. Your wife is a beautiful woman and you are a very lucky man. There is only one thing I cannot understand," continued Owl, "and that is the terrible foxy smell in this igloo."

Mavarana looked at Raven in horror. She ran over to the bed and from beneath it pulled out her fox skin. She put it on and ran out of the igloo.

Raven ran out after Mavarana and called to her. He told her how much he loved her, and that he wanted her to be with him for the rest of her life. But Mavarana ran very quickly. Raven dashed back to the igloo, put on his wing-cape, and flew off in search of her. He flew across the land and searched everywhere. But Mavarana had disappeared, and Raven was very sad. He returned to the igloo, and found Owl munching away on the seal meat that he had brought home.

Raven watched Owl eating, and as he watched, anger welled up within him. The blood rushed to his head, and he cried out at Owl, "You frazzle-feathered, long-beaked, flea-bitten idiot! You're all mouth – your mouth is so big that when you open it I can see right through to the other end!" And even though Raven was sweet-tempered and kind, the tips of his wings curled up and he gave Owl a tremendous smash in the face. Owl flew backwards, bounced off the wall of the igloo, flew to the other side, hit the wall and just hung there, his feet dangling and his beak stuck deep in the snow wall. Raven tugged at Owl and finally pulled him out of the wall.

Owl stared at Raven and said, "Why did you hit me? All I said was that there's an awful foxy smell in the igloo."

Fury again engulfed Raven and again he hit Owl, muttering, "You ignorant, draggle-tailed, slow-witted fool!" Raven hit Owl so hard that Owl flew backwards, bounced off the wall, flew forward, hit the opposite wall with a thud, and collapsed onto the ground. Raven ran over to Owl and picked him up. He couldn't believe what he saw! Owl's face was flat, and his beak was pushed in. Just two big, round eyes stared out at him. Raven had hit Owl so hard that his face was now flat.

And from that time on, Owls have always had flat faces.

Raven Recovers
Light For His People

Long after Raven had created the world, an evil, selfish man became chief of an Eskimo village. His name was Tupilak. He was not happy to share the world with other men, but wanted all the beautiful things in the world to belong to him alone.

One day, Tupilak decided to steal the sun and the moon and the stars. He fashioned three jugs out of clay and made a tight-fitting cover for each. Early that evening, as the sun was setting, he took one of the jugs and ran to the end of the earth. He caught the falling sun in his jug and then quickly put the cover on it. That night, as the moon moved down the sky towards the horizon, he again ran to the end of the earth. He caught the falling moon in his second jug and quickly covered it. The stars grieved for the sun and the moon, and they fell down from the sky. Whenever he saw a falling star, Tupilak ran and caught it in his third jug. Soon all the stars were in the jug and he covered it.

The people in all the other villages were miserable. They prayed for the return of the light of the sun and the moon and the stars. People groped about in darkness, and it was hard to hunt and find food. The people craved the sun and the moon, and they remembered with sadness the beauty of the twinkling stars. They often met to talk about ways to bring light back to all the people.

Raven lived in one of the dark villages, and he felt sorrow for his people. The chief of his village was a kind and wise man, who wanted all the people to share the good things on earth. One day the village chief said, "I have two beautiful daughters. The man who brings light back to our people may choose whichever one he wishes."

The strongest and most skilled men in the village went after the light. One after another, they left their village in search of the sun and the moon and the stars, but no one ever came back.

After many brave men had been lost, Raven stood up in the presence of the entire village. "Listen to me!" he called out.

His voice boomed out among the people, and they all turned toward him.

"I have seen my people suffer," Raven cried, "and my heart is heavy with grief. Evil has been done to us, and we must fight the one who has brought us such misery. I promise you: I will bring back the sun and the moon and the stars!"

Raven drew his feather-cape over his shoulders, pulled down his beak, and sailed up into the air. For a long time he flew in darkness, and then he saw a faint light in the sky. The farther he went, the lighter it became, and, when he reached Tupilak's village, the light was so strong that it almost blinded him.

The light radiated out of a large tent in the centre of the village, and Raven knew that the tent contained the sun and the moon and the stars. He waited on a nearby cliff until the sunlight was gone and watched as the moonlight shone brightly out of the tent. The people slept. Raven hopped off his perch and flew silently into the tent. But Tupilak lay on his bed with one eye open. When he saw Raven, he leaped up and screamed, "Get away, you thief. The light is mine, and no one will steal it from me."

Tupilak picked up a huge stick and tried to hit Raven. Raven flew back and forth, dodging each swing of the stick, but he could not get near the jugs. Finally, with a mighty sweep of his wings, he soared out of the tent. He flew back to the cliff and perched on its highest peak. There, while he was staring at the moonlight that glowed out of the chief's tent, he began to develop his plan.

Near the village was a stream, and the next morning Raven flew above the stream and watched the women as they came for water. Soon he saw a beautifully dressed young woman, and he realized that she must be Tupilak's daughter. She carried a ladle and dipped out some water. As she drank, Raven cast a magic spell and changed himself into a tiny feather. He floated down and down, and fell into the ladle. The young woman failed to see the floating feather and swallowed it with the water. She coughed, and then ran home to tell her husband that she had swallowed some strange thing while drinking at the stream.

"Don't worry about it," said her husband. "It was probably your imagination."

Many months later, the woman gave birth to a son. It was Raven, and he had the form of a little baby. Being the first child, he was fondled and nursed tenderly. His mother and father loved him, and his grandfather, Tupilak, adored him. Whatever Raven saw, he called for; and whatever he called for was given to him. If it was not given to him immediately, he cried and pestered until he got it. In this way he handled everything in the house, except the three little jugs which were kept on a high shelf.

Raven watched as the chief opened each jug. When he opened one, the sun shone brilliantly and made day for the village. Then he covered the jug and opened the other two, and there were moonbeams and starlight.

Raven grew to be a strong and healthy baby. But even though he cried and behaved like a baby, he had Raven's mind.

One day, one of his mother's helpers saw a bump on his forehead. "Poor baby," she cried, "you fell on your head. I will put ice on it." Each day she put ice on the bump on Raven's forehead, but it grew and grew.

Raven knew that the bump was his beak and he worried. "How long will it be," he wondered, "before they know what it is?"

Whenever Raven saw little feathers, he cried for them and they were given to him. When he was alone, he wove them together and made himself a little wing-cape. Then he hid it under his blankets.

One day, while Tupilak was having his afternoon nap, Raven crawled onto the bed and lay down beside him.

"The jugs! the jugs!" Raven suddenly cried out. "Let me play with the jugs on the shelf!"

"No!" said his mother. "No one but your grandfather can touch those jugs!"

"I want them! Give them to me! I want them!" he cried, and began to scream and kick.

Tupilak woke up with a start, unaware of the cause of all the noise. "Oh, give him anything he wants," he shouted angrily, "and tell him to shut up!" And he went back to sleep.

Two little jugs were handed to Raven and he opened each one. In the first he saw the stars. The second contained the moon. The third, from which the sun shone brilliantly, remained on the shelf. Raven played with the two jugs and practised opening and closing them until he could replace each lid with a single, swift motion. Then he pushed the jugs aside casually, as though they were merely another toy. But he was careful not to let the moon or the stars spill out of them.

A few days later, when no one was around, Raven put on his wing-cape and lowered his beak over his mouth. He flew up to the shelf, and grasped two jugs in his claws. With his beak, he covered the third one that contained the sun, lifted it up, and flew out of Tupilak's tent.

The moment the village was plunged into darkness, Tupilak ran toward his tent, shouting, "My jugs! My jugs!" As he ran, he fell into the village stream, and was carried away. He was never seen again.

Raven flew for many days until, finally, he arrived at his village. He called all the people together, and opened one of the jugs. The stars poured out of the jug and streamed to their places in the sky. Then he opened the second jug, and the moon rose up rapidly to join the stars. The people were wild with joy!

Raven waited for the people's eyes to grow accustomed to the light. Then he opened the third jug, and the sun flowed out of it, rose up, and shone brilliantly in the sky. The villagers were overwhelmed with joy, and began to sing and shout and dance.

Then the village Chief called together his two young daughters, who looked at Raven with adoration and respect. While the villagers celebrated the return of light, Raven married the Chief's eldest daughter. He rejoiced when he saw how proud and content she was.

Raven and his wife lived together for many happy years.

His wife grew older and more graceful, and each day he came to love her more. He wished that he could grow old with her, but he stayed as young as he had been the day he created the world.

One day, Raven's wife died. Raven wept as he carried her out of the igloo and placed her on the frozen ground. He covered her with large rocks so that people would always know where Raven's wife lay buried. Then, weeping silently and sadly, he swept his feather-cape across his shoulders, lowered his beak, and flew away from the village he had known and loved for so many years.

Raven
And The Children

The wind howled past Raven as he walked slowly across the fields of ice and snow. He held his harpoon in one hand and pulled a frozen seal with the other. The snowfields stretched endlessly around him. He was hungry and tired, but there was no sign of life and he walked on. The stars shimmered and he stopped to look at them, to be sure that he was walking in the right direction. The moonbeams danced on the snowbanks. It was so cold that tears came to his eyes,

and the light sparkled and shone and made star-shaped patterns.

As Raven walked, clouds moved across the sky, and snow began to fall. The wind whistled past his face, and he walked faster to escape the coming storm.

Raven stopped for a moment and strained to see a distant light on the horizon. He smiled and hurried on. As he came closer, he saw his igloo, with the light of the oil lamp shining through the ice windows. He was hungry, and began to eat soon after he stepped into the igloo.

Raven ate slowly and, as he chewed the frozen seal meat, he looked out the ice windows of his igloo and watched the

raging storm. The snow flew past, circled, and swirled around. As Raven peered out, he saw movement. He rubbed his eyes in disbelief, and looked again. Five little forms were moving out in the snow. Raven suddenly realized that they were children. He ran out and led them into his igloo. The children had been lost in the blizzard, and they were cold and hungry. Raven threw his wing-cape around them and poured a little more oil into the lamp to provide heat. The lamp flame brightened, and Raven examined the children's anxious faces.

"Don't worry," Raven said gently. "The blizzard will soon pass." And he stretched his arms toward the children to embrace them, to warm and console them.

The children reared back, and stared at Raven in awe and fear.

"Who are you?" the oldest child asked.

"Why do you have a beak on your forehead?" asked another. "And what is this huge, black feather-blanket covering us?"

Raven was worried. If he told the children who he was, they would fear him even more.

"Sit down, children," he said, "and I will tell you a story about Raven and the Weasel."

"There was once a silly old Raven," he began, "who was very hungry. He floated across the sky, searching for food on the ice and snow."

The children listened, became absorbed in the story, and settled themselves around Raven.

"Raven saw seals and walruses basking in the sunshine," he continued, "but he looked for something daintier and tastier. As Raven flew on, he saw some bushes growing at the side of a stream. He flew closer and then suddenly saw a weasel drinking. Raven's mouth watered at the thought of a tasty little weasel.

"The moment the weasel caught sight of Raven, it dashed across the ground towards its den. But Raven saw the den, flew in front of the weasel, and blocked the entrance.

"The weasel looked at Raven and said, 'Well, I guess you've caught me! I'm very fat, and you will have a good meal. Go ahead and eat me! But if you wish to celebrate before you eat, then I will sing while you dance!'

"Raven looked at the weasel and saw that he was indeed fat and beautiful, and realized what a delicious meal he would make.

"Weasel looked at Raven and said, 'Don't be embarrassed. I am proud that I shall be eaten by Raven the great dancer, because I have heard that you are a very fine dancer. Now, if you will dance, I will sing, and then you can eat me!'

"Raven was pleased to hear the weasel say such nice things about him.

" 'Please,' begged the weasel, 'please dance for me because I have only one wish before you eat me: I wish to see you dance!'

"This pleased Raven so much that he agreed to dance.

"So the weasel sang:

'Oh, Raven, Raven, how well you dance,
Oh, Raven, Raven, how nicely you prance,
Your eyes are radiant,
Your beak's like a lance,
Oh, Raven, Raven, how well you dance.'

"Then they stopped to rest and Weasel said, 'I am very pleased with your wonderful dancing, but I have heard that you can dance even greater dances. So please, before you eat me, dance your very best. Now I will sing once more, so shut your eyes and dance.'

"Raven closed his eyes and hopped clumsily about while Weasel sang:

'Oh, Raven, Raven, look up at the sky,
As you do your beautiful dance,
Kick your legs high,
And make your wings fly,
As you do your beautiful dance.'

"The moment Raven kicked his legs and spread out his wings, the weasel ran right under him and disappeared into his burrow.

"Raven stopped dancing and stared at the weasel's den. Suddenly Weasel's little nose appeared and Weasel sang this song:

'Oh, Raven, Raven, what a fool you are,
Oh, Raven, Raven, how vain you are,

You're incredibly dumb,
Your brain's in your bum,
Oh, Raven, Raven, what a fool you are.' "

The children laughed as Raven finished his story.

Raven felt happiness well up within him. "There is nothing more beautiful," he thought, "than happy children's faces."

"Who is Raven?" one of the children asked.

Raven scanned their eager faces.

"I am Raven," he said.

The children laughed.

"Yes! I really am!" said Raven. He lowered his beak over his mouth, swirled his wing-cape around his shoulders, and stretched out his wings.

The children drew back in terror.

Raven lifted his beak up to his forehead, took off his wing-cape, and a smile radiated across his face.

The children laughed and drew close to Raven. They surrounded him and hugged him.

The children soon grew tired, and their heads nodded with sleepiness. Raven tucked them under the blankets, and spent all that night watching them. Little hands lay on top of the blankets, and Raven examined each set of five fingers. "Five," he thought, "is a magic number."

The next day the sun shone brightly when Raven and the children emerged from the igloo. The world was beautiful! The snow sparkled in the sunlight and looked like a sheet of dancing flame. The rich blue sky looked cool and majestic.

Raven was overawed by the beauty that surrounded him. "I created the world long ago," he thought, "and all by itself it developed a splendour I never dreamed of."

Raven and the children travelled all day until they finally arrived at a large village. The children were swept into their parents' arms, and Raven was welcomed warmly by the village chief. The children begged Raven to stay, and he made his home with them. The children loved Raven and rarely thought of him as the Creator. But when they noticed the beak on his forehead, they were always a little afraid.

Raven
And The Spirit

R aven loved the children in his village and he stayed with them for many years. His wisdom and kindness became known across the land, and people always sought him out. No man or woman ever left his igloo without enjoying his hospitality. He gave food to the poor, he cured sick people with magic herbs, and he gave advice and encouragement to all who came to him.

One day a man came running from a far-away village.

"Help us, Raven," he cried. "Our village is haunted by a spirit, and we are frightened. Our Shaman, who is the best witch-doctor in this whole area, says every prayer he knows without avail."

"Have you seen the spirit?" asked Raven.

"No, never," said the man.

"What does he do?" asked Raven.

"At night," replied the man, "when we settle down to sleep, and our igloos are quiet, there is suddenly a groaning noise, and a whirlwind roars through one of the igloos. Sometimes the wind is so terrible that the top of the igloo flies off."

"What does the groaning noise sound like?" asked Raven.

"It says 'Yes-no-yes-no-yes-no,'" said the man.

"Does your village Shaman talk to the spirit?" Raven asked.

"Yes," said the man. "Our Shaman calls to the spirit in the name of the powerful sea-goddess Sedna. He says the holiest prayers and then asks, 'Are you there? What do you want from us? Will you leave us?' And the spirit says only 'Yes-no-yes-no-yes-no.'"

So Raven joined the man and went to his village. He searched all around until, finally, he saw something that no mere mortal could see – he saw the spirit! It was fast asleep in the Shaman's igloo.

Raven asked to be left alone. When all was silent, he tip-toed to the spirit and tapped his shoulder.

The spirit suddenly leaped up, startled, and started to cry for help.

"Calm yourself," said Raven soothingly. "I am Raven, and I am here to help you."

The spirit wept. "My name is Samik, and I am lost," he said. "I left the body of a man a few weeks ago, and now I'm searching for a new body."

"Don't you like to transmigrate into new bodies?" asked Raven. "It's exciting! What pleasure the first weeks are, when you discover the marvellous things you can do."

"I know, I know," said the spirit. "I've transmigrated before. But now I can't make up my mind on what I want to be – a man or a woman, a bird or a wolf."

"It's wonderful to be a bird," said Raven. "What power I feel when I soar through the air. Would you like to be a bird?"

"Yes-no-yes-no-yes-no," cried the spirit. "Yes! It would be fun to be a bird, but then again, no! It might not be."

"How about a whale?" asked Raven. "Think of the joy of floating through the water, the biggest and most powerful animal in the world, with only friends and no enemies. Would you like to be a whale?"

"Yes!" cried the spirit. "It would be a joy to be a whale, but then again, no! It might not be."

"Would you like to be a pretty girl with long black braids and shiny white teeth?" asked Raven.

"Yes!" cried Samik, and his head shook up and down. Then he cried, "No!" and his head shook from side to side. And as he exclaimed yes-no-yes-no-yes-no, his head shook up and down and from side to side so quickly that soon it went round and round.

Samik's head whirled around faster, and then his body began to twirl. Soon Raven saw him lift off and grabbed him before he could get too far.

Raven thought for a little while.

"Aha!" he exclaimed, "I know exactly what to do! There is a Shaman in a village not far from here who has so little character and such a tiny spirit that there is plenty of room for you to transmigrate into his body."

So Raven took Samik by the hand and they flew off to the village. When Raven caught sight of the Shaman mumbling at the people around him, he turned Samik toward the Shaman, pushed him, and in a flash Samik entered the Shaman's body.

The people were stunned when their dull, witless Shaman suddenly leapt up and started to yell "Yes-no-yes-no-yes-no." Then he got up and marched in one direction, turned around and marched in the other, then started to twirl around in circles.

"Our Shaman is having a holy whirling fit!" one man shouted.

"He has been possessed by a great holy spirit," called another.

And they ran off to tell the people.

The Shaman in whose body Samik now lived became famous among the people in all the surrounding villages. His wisdom was the greatest they knew or heard of. When a man needed luck to hunt seals, he called on Samik to plead with the great goddess Sedna, who lives at the bottom of the sea. Then Samik would stand up, his head circling around and his

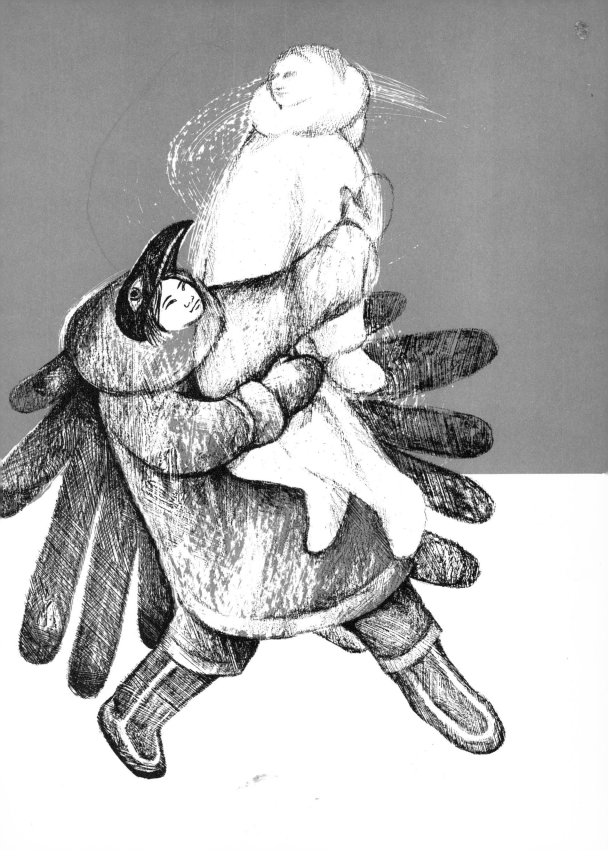

body trembling, and he would call, "Yes-no-yes-no-yes-no!" And the people stood in awe that Samik should have so intimate a conversation with a goddess. And when he came out of his trance, the man would ask, "What did Sedna say? Will I catch seals tomorrow?"

And Samik chanted, "Tomorrow you will catch a seal, but then again, maybe you will not."

Another man would say, "My wife is possessed by an evil spirit, and she yells at me all the time. When will she stop screaming at me?"

And Samik would say, "She will stop tomorrow, but then again, maybe she will not."

Samik's fame spread to distant lands. He was always right, and never, never made a wrong prediction. Anyone who could prophesy so perfectly, the people reasoned, must indeed be in touch with the gods. The people brought Samik the choicest food, and he married the prettiest girl. He was revered and loved by his people. And he, in turn, loved all the holy spirits, but above all he loved Raven for his wisdom and goodness.

Raven
Leaves The World

For many years, Raven lived with the people whose children he had saved. The village was a happy one, and all the people shared the food they caught. One day when food was being served in the community hut, a very tall, strong man entered and took all the food away. No one resisted him.

"Why did no one fight him?" asked Raven.

The chief turned to Raven and said, "That man is the son of an evil witch who lives in another village. His name is

Axsuq. We are afraid of him, for his mother gave him a bear which is powerful enough to kill any man. He travels from village to village, steals food, and hurts whomever he wishes."

The next day, Raven went hunting. As he was carrying his seals home, Axsuq suddenly appeared and demanded a seal. Raven refused, and the evil man walked away in anger.

That night, a villager, who was very frightened and excited, came running to Raven's house.

"Raven, Raven," he called, "Axsuq has challenged you to fight him tomorrow."

The chief begged Raven not to go, but Raven was determined to fight. He sat up late that night and made a strong spear. Then he carved a bow and many arrows.

In the morning, when Raven stepped out of his igloo, he saw Axsuq walking toward him. The two men stood and faced each other for a long time. Neither said anything.

Axsuq began to move backwards, and Raven followed him. Raven's wing-cape hung loosely around his shoulders and it billowed out in the wind as he walked. The powerful beak on his forehead jutted out like a knife as he moved. Axsuq moved slowly and then, suddenly, he whistled. When Raven turned around to look, he saw a huge polar bear running toward him.

Raven stood perfectly still until the bear was almost on top of him. Then he quickly stepped aside, and, as the bear moved past him, he plunged his spear through the bear. It fell over and died.

As soon as Axsuq saw what happened, he put an arrow in

his bow and took aim. But Raven was too quick. He shot his arrow first and hit Axsuq. Although Axsuq was wounded, he kept on shooting. But he got weaker and weaker, and his arrows lost their force. Then Raven shot again and killed Axsuq.

When Raven was sure that Axsuq was dead, he came forward and called loudly, "Let all who want to take Axsuq's part come and fight with me." No one came.

But there was one man who ran from the village, secretly, to tell Axsuq's mother, who was an evil witch.

The next morning, a messenger arrived at the village. He was sent by Axsuq's mother, and the message was simple. She wanted revenge and she challenged Raven to meet her.

All morning the people waited. Then they heard the sound of crunching snow, and they could see the evil witch coming over a hillcrest. They gasped when they saw a huge, terrible serpent crawling beside her on the ground. The serpent came down the hill and into the village.

The evil witch stood beside the serpent and looked at the villagers. Then she called out, "Listen to me, Raven! This serpent is an evil spirit. He, and many like him, are the messengers of Death. He is stronger than you are! He conquers all that cross his path. He attacks every living thing and always wins! You, Raven, are a coward. You hide behind your Raven-beak, your immortality. Take it off! Cast off your wing-cape, your cloak of godhood, and become a real man. Courage is a man's quality, not yours! Let us see how brave you are! Be a man and fight!"

"No, Raven!" cried the chief. "Don't listen to her."

Raven took off his wing-cape. Then he gripped the beak on his forehead and, with a sudden twist, lifted it off. He gave both to the chief, who held them in awe.

The witch smiled, and her face was evil. She pointed to Raven and said to the serpent, "There is the man you are to kill!"

The serpent crawled toward Raven. It opened its great mouth and raised its head high above the ground. Its long forked tongue lashed out as it slithered toward Raven. It came closer and closer, and, when it lunged, Raven leapt aside

sharply. The serpent slashed with its tail, but Raven leapt over it.

Suddenly, for the first time, Raven felt fear! He was terrified as the serpent turned around to begin its new attack. His muscles froze when he realized that he was weak, mortal, human – that he could die in this one encounter with the serpent. And there was no escape, for the serpent moved faster than he did.

But as Raven faced the serpent there developed within him a sense of courage and purpose that he had never felt before. An inner strength surged through him, and Raven stepped forward boldly, upright, ready to fight.

The serpent lunged at Raven with his gaping mouth and lashed at him with his tail. Each time the serpent struck, Raven leaped aside, but the serpent came at him again. As he fought, Raven saw that the joints of the serpent's body were soft while the rest of its body was as hard as rock and no spear could stab through it. Raven continued to jump back and forth, avoiding the serpent's tail each time it lashed out at him. Then, taking careful aim, he raised his spear and stabbed the serpent's joints. Blood spurted out, but still the serpent fought on. Raven speared the serpent again and again, and, as all the people watched, the serpent gradually weakened. Its evil power was sapped and finally it lunged toward Raven, shuddered, and died. At that moment the witch screamed, shrivelled up, and vanished.

The people cheered and then they grew silent.

Raven walked slowly to the chief. He took his wing-cape

and swept it around his shoulders. He put his beak near his forehead and, with a little twist, set it in place.

Raven turned toward the children and smiled at them. He plucked feathers from his wing-cape and blew on them, and his magic breath turned each feather into a little wing-cape for each child.

"Never forget me!" he told the children. "I created the World, and I gave you Life. It all began with me. But the future lies with you!"

Raven flew up and hovered above the village. The warm sun melted the snow, and the streams of water flowed to the rivers. The northern mosses and plants were green, and the gaily coloured berries grew abundantly on the bushes. People lived in harmony with each other, and the animals roamed across the land, the sea, and the sky.

Raven knew that what he had created was good, and that now he was no longer needed. Wings outswept, he glided five full circles over the village. Then he gathered speed and flew off. He was never seen again.

The Eskimo people have never forgotten Raven. His spirit, his love of life, his search for happiness live on forever in the people he created. To this day, when there is a feast, or when people are gathered together to wait out a long, terrible blizzard, a great storyteller rises and says, "Listen to me, for now I will tell you the story of Raven." A hush falls over the gathering, and the storyteller raises his arms, and chants, "In the beginning, there was only Raven and the falling snow-flakes. . ."

Acknowledgements

The ten stories in this book were chosen from hundreds of Eskimo legends and folktales that have been recorded by anthropologists and explorers. Because Eskimo life is so different from our own, it was necessary to retell the stories in a way that would appeal to children in our culture. Wherever it was possible, however, portions of the stories were left unchanged, in order to retain the flavour of the Eskimo tale.

The stories are derived from the following sources: F. BOAS, "Eskimo of Baffin Land and Hudson Bay," *Bulletin of the American Museum of Natural History*, vol. 15, 1901; F.A. GOLDER, "Tales from Kodiak Island," *Journal of American Folklore*, vol. 16, 1903; A. L. KROEBER, "Animal Tales of the Eskimo," *Journal of American Folklore*, vol. 12, 1899; E. W. NELSON, "The Eskimo about Bering Strait," *Eighteenth Annual Report of the Bureau of American Ethnology*, 1899; KNUD RASMUSSEN, *The People of the Polar North* (London: Kegan Paul, Trench, Trubner and Co., 1908); KNUD RASMUSSEN, "The Netsilik Eskimo," *Report of the Fifth Thule Expedition*, vol. 8 (Copenhagen: Gyldendal, 1931); KNUD RASMUSSEN, "The Alaskan Eskimos," *Report of the Fifth Thule Expedition*, vol. 10 (Copenhagen: Gyldendal, 1933); R. F. SPENCER, "The North Alaskan Eskimo," *Bureau of American Ethnology*, Bulletin 171 (Smithsonian Institution Press, 1959).

I am grateful to the heirs of Knud Rasmussen, to Gyldendal Publishing Company, and to Routledge and Kegan Paul Limited for permission to retell "The Creation," "The Raven who was Anxious to be Married," "The Raven and the Goose," and "The Two Shamans who Crashed in the Air" ("Raven And The Keewak Bird"). The story "Raven Leaves The World" is adapted from "The Worm" (pp. 414-417 in "The North Alaskan Eskimo") with the kind permission of the author, Dr. Robert F. Spencer, and the Smithsonian Institution Press. It is a pleasure to thank Miss Nora Corley, Librarian of the Arctic Institute of North America, for making many of these volumes available to me.

This book was designed by David-John Shaw